BEN'S WEST TEXAS ★SNOW★

Written By Callie Metler-Smith

Illustrated by Christee Curran-Bauer

Ben Metler

Sandra's
Family:
I hope
you enjoy
Ben's Adventure!
Callie Metler-Smith

Ben's West Texas Snow

SUMMARY – Ben longs to see snow in West Texas — like the one he's seen on T.V. Just when he thinks he never will, he visits Pop on the cotton farm and discovers a special kind of "snow" that's equally beautiful and fascinating.

Clear Fork Publishing
P.O. Box 870 - 102 S. Swenson
Stamford, Texas 79553
(325)773-5550 - www.clearforkpublishing.com

Printed and Bound in the United States of America.

Hardcover ISBN - 978-1-946101-83-9

Pop-Pop, thank you so much for sharing your West Texas Cotton Farm
with me and my boys.
I will never forget how the world of cotton farming has shaped my life.
For Lynne Marie, Melissa, and Rosie, thank you for being my soul sisters and dealing
with the endless edits and moments of excitement.
I'm so grateful that you are part of my writing journey.
Christee, thank you taking my book baby and adding your own stamp of beauty on it.
Mom, thank you for being my biggest cheerleader. XOXO - Callie

To my family and my husband, Russ, for your years of support. - Christee

Ben loved growing up in West Texas.

He liked hiding in the coolness of his dirt fort when

the West Texas sun became so hot it cracked the earth.

He relished cooling off with fresh, juicy watermelon from Grammy's garden, and then having a seed spitting contest with his brother.

He enjoyed fishing for catfish at Lake Stamford with Pop, even when they became hot and sweaty and didn't get a bite.

He loved everything about his West Texas farm life, until he realized . . .

It hardly ever snowed!

He stared at the big blue Texas sky, watched billowing clouds roll by, and wondered why.

"Mom, do you know why it doesn't snow here?"

Mom sighed. "Ben, it's just too hot in our part of Texas."

He asked his grammy. "Will I ever get to see snow?"

Grammy looked up from her canning jars and frowned. "When pigs fly."

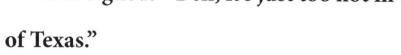

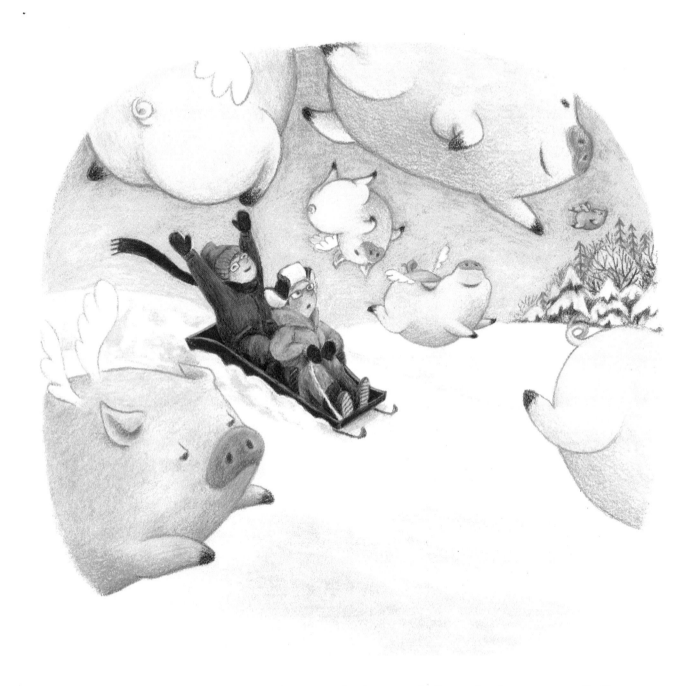

Ben thought about that for a while, and decided to go ask Pop.

"Pop, do you know why it doesn't snow here?"

Pop tipped his hat back and thought a moment.

"Now who told you that?" He asked.

"Mom and Grammy," Ben explained.

"Well, they're half wrong," Pop said. "Come with me."

Ben followed as Pop grabbed some seed and loaded up the planters on his tractor.

Side by side, they spread cottonseed
up and down the plowed rows.

"Will I see snow now?" Ben asked.

"Not yet," said Pop. "We must be patient."

For the next several days, they seeded the fields.

Still, no snow.

When he was done, Ben looked at Pop.

"Pop, I don't see any snow."

"Just wait, Ben." Pop said.

Weeks went by . . .

Ben waited and waited.

"It's never going to snow," Ben said to his mom.

"If Pop says it's so, then it must be so," she replied.

Finally, plants poked through the ground, their stick-like arms reaching toward the sky.

They had little flowers on them that were white and
little green leaf patterns that Pop called squares.

But still, no snow.

The cotton plants sprouted and grew bigger and bigger. Ben watched

balls form on the ends like little hands. Pop called these cotton bolls.

But still, no snow.

Weeks later, Pop looked out over the field and wiped the sweat from his forehead.

Frost came, the green plants turned brown. The cotton bolls opened and puffs of cotton peeked through.

Ben inspected the field. "I still don't see any snow, Pop."

Pop gazed approvingly at the rows of brown bushes.

"Soon."

The weather started to get a little colder,

which reminded Ben of the seasons the rest of the country enjoyed, and snow.

"The snow must surely be arriving soon," Ben told Pop.

"Why don't we just go see?" asked Pop.

Ben ran toward the fields. There it was -- row after row of fluffy cotton and it looked just like soft, white, fluffy snow!

Ben called to his mom and grammy.

"Look, Pop did it! He made it snow in West Texas, and it goes on for miles!"

"Now that's what I call a West Texas snow," said Pop.

"It's the best snow of all," said Ben.

The Real Pop and Ben

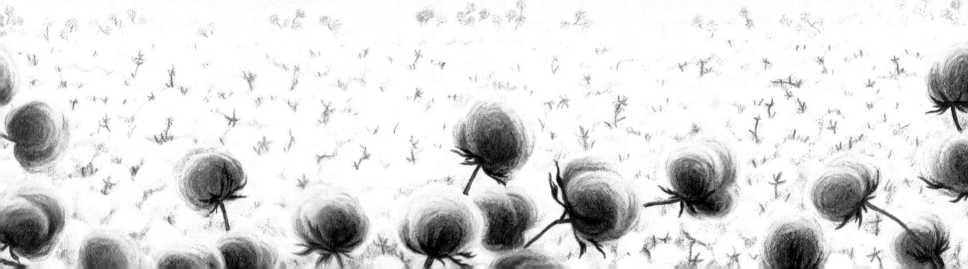

Author's Note

Growing up in West Texas, I was always in awe of the snow that fell in other parts of the country. While it might snow once in a blue moon, it didn't stick or last more than a few hours. One day, I realized that cotton fields looked like a blanket of snow and were just as beautiful and fascinating as the real thing.

It is impossible to live in a small farming community such as Stamford without seeing cotton or learning about the cotton trade. Starting in late fall, empty lots in town start filling with cotton bales waiting to be processed by the local gin. Most West Texas cotton farming is called dry-land farming. This makes cotton farmers dependent on rain to provide the much-needed moisture for their plants. Most years are either really plentiful or really sparse, depending on the amount of rain the crop receives. Cotton has been a major industry in West Texas since the early 1900s, and Texas leads the United States in the production of Cotton. Cotton is the state's leading cash crop and over 6 million acres of cotton is planted each year.

Callie Metler-Smith is the owner of Clear Fork Media Group in Stamford, Texas. She grew up on a cotton farm in Jones County that has been owned by her family for over 100 years and spent many summers going up and down cotton rows checking to make sure they were weed free. When not working on her corner of the Stamford Square, she is spending time with her husband, Philip and two sons, Logan and Ben.

Christee Curran-Bauer graduated from Pratt Institute with a BFA in Illustration. She was born and raised in New Jersey and currently lives in Virginia Beach, Virginia with her husband and French bulldog. She has never been to West Texas, but would love to see the "Snow of the South" in person one day.

CPSIA information can be obtained at www.ICGtesting.com
Printed in the USA
BVIW12n2338211018
530276BV00005B/18